Date: 2/21/18

J 796.334 CHE
Stewart, Mark,
Chelsea F. C. /

PALM BEACH COUNTY
LIBRARY SYSTEM
3650 SUMMIT BLVD.
WEST PALM BEACH, FL 33406

CHELSEA F.C.

By
Mark Stewart

Chicago, Illinois

NorwoodHouse Press

P.O. Box 316598 • Chicago, Illinois 60631
For more information about Norwood House Press please visit our website at
www.norwoodhousepress.com or call 866-565-2900.

Photography and Collectibles:
The trading cards and other memorabilia assembled in the background for this book's cover and interior pages are all part of the author's collection and are reproduced for educational and artistic purposes.

All photos courtesy of Associated Press except the following individual photos and artifacts (page numbers):
Rafo/Mostar (6), A&BC Chewing Gum Ltd. (10 top), Cadet Sweets/Gee Products (10 bottom),
Longacre Press Ltd. (11 top), F.K.S. Publishers Ltd. (11 middle), Author's Collection (11 bottom),
Futera Trade Cards Ltd. (16), Topps, Inc. (23).

Cover image: Associated Press, (Rex Features via AP Images)

Designer: Ron Jaffe
Series Editor: Mike Kennedy
Content Consultants: Michael Jacobsen and Jonathan Wentworth-Ping
Project Management: Black Book Partners, LLC
Editorial Production: Lisa Walsh

LIBRARY OF CONGRESS CATALOGING-IN-PUBLICATION DATA
Names: Stewart, Mark, 1960 July 7- author.
Title: Chelsea F. C. / By Mark Stewart.
Description: Chicago Illinois : Norwood House Press, 2017. | Series: First
   Touch Soccer | Includes bibliographical references and index. | Audience:
   Age 5-8. | Audience: K to Grade 3.
Identifiers: LCCN 2016058199 (print) | LCCN 2017002179 (ebook) | ISBN
   9781599538587 (library edition : alk. paper) | ISBN 9781684040773 (eBook)
Subjects: LCSH: Chelsea Football Club--History--Juvenile literature.
Classification: LCC GV943.6.C44 S84 2017 (print) | LCC GV943.6.C44 (ebook) |
   DDC 796.334/640941--dc23
LC record available at https://lccn.loc.gov/2016058199

©2018 by Norwood House Press. All rights reserved.
No part of this book may be reproduced without written permission from the publisher.

This publication is intended for educational purposes and is not affiliated with any team, league, or association including: Chelsea Football Club, the English Premier League, The Union of European Football Associations (UEFA), or the Federation Internationale de Football Association (FIFA).

302N--072017
Manufactured in the United States of America in North Mankato, Minnesota.

Contents

Meet Chelsea F.C. 5
Time Machine 6
Best Seat in the House 9
Collector's Corner 10
Worthy Opponents 12
Club Ways 14
On the Map 16
Kit and Crest 19
We Won! 20
For the Record 22
Soccer Words 24
Index 24
About the Author 24

Words in **bold type** are defined on page 24.

In soccer, star players often go by a one-word nickname. In this book, we use the nickname followed by the player's (*full name*).

Chelsea captain John Terry lets the fans know he hears them after a victory in 2016.

Meet Chelsea F.C.

If you see a photo of a famous player in a blue uniform, chances are he plays for the Chelsea Football Club. In most parts of the world, when people say "football" they are talking about the game of soccer, not American football.

Chelsea players are nicknamed The Blues. They are known for their grace and power. They come from all over the world to test their skill and play with the best.

Time Machine

In 1905, a man named Gus Mears started the Chelsea Football Club in a neighborhood of West London. His family owned the team for more than 70 years and put many great players on the field.

After many years of ups and downs, Chelsea became one of the best teams in the world. The club's great players include Jimmy Greaves, **Frank Lampard**, and Didier Drogba.

FRANK LAMPARD

Didier Drogba gets ready to make a move on a defender during a 2007 match. Drogba was an amazing scorer for the club.

For every seat that is sold at Stamford Bridge, another fan is turned away. That is why Chelsea needed to enlarge its stadium.

Best Seat in the House

Chelsea plays on a field called Stamford Bridge. It is one of the oldest stadiums in England and is loved by fans and players. Peter Osgood, one of the club's great stars, had his ashes buried under the stands after he died. The stadium holds more than 40,000 fans and will soon hold more than 60,000.

Collector's Corner

These collectibles show some of the best Chelsea players ever.

Peter Sillett

Defender
1953–1962
Sillett was one of the best defensive players of the 1950s. He was a hard **tackler** and had a booming shot.

Jimmy Greaves

Striker
1957–1961
Greaves was a goal-scoring machine. It was a sad day for Chelsea fans when the club sold him to A.C. Milan.

Peter Osgood

Striker
1964–1974 & 1978–1979
Osgood was one of the game's smartest players. If a defense had a weakness, he was sure to find it.

Charlie Cooke

Forward
1966–1972 & 1974–1978
Cooke brought fans to their feet whenever he touched the ball. His dribbling and passing were magical.

Didier Drogba

Striker
2004–2012 & 2014–2015
Drogba was a super scorer. Chelsea won its first **Premier League** title in 50 seasons the year he joined the club.

Worthy Opponents

The city of London has many soccer clubs. The closer the clubs, the better the rivalries. Chelsea's main rivals are Arsenal and Tottenham Hotspur. Both play in North London. Chelsea and Arsenal are often the city's two best clubs. Fans get excited about their matches. The matches against Tottenham also draw sellout crowds.

Andre Schurrle squeezes off a shot between two Arsenal players during a match at Stamford Bridge.

Club Ways

Have you ever heard of a magic number? For Chelsea players and fans, number 9 is the opposite of a magic number. For more than 20 years, the players wearing this number have not done very well. Some have played poorly. Others have been injured. On most teams, number 9 is very popular. Few Chelsea players are brave enough to wear it!

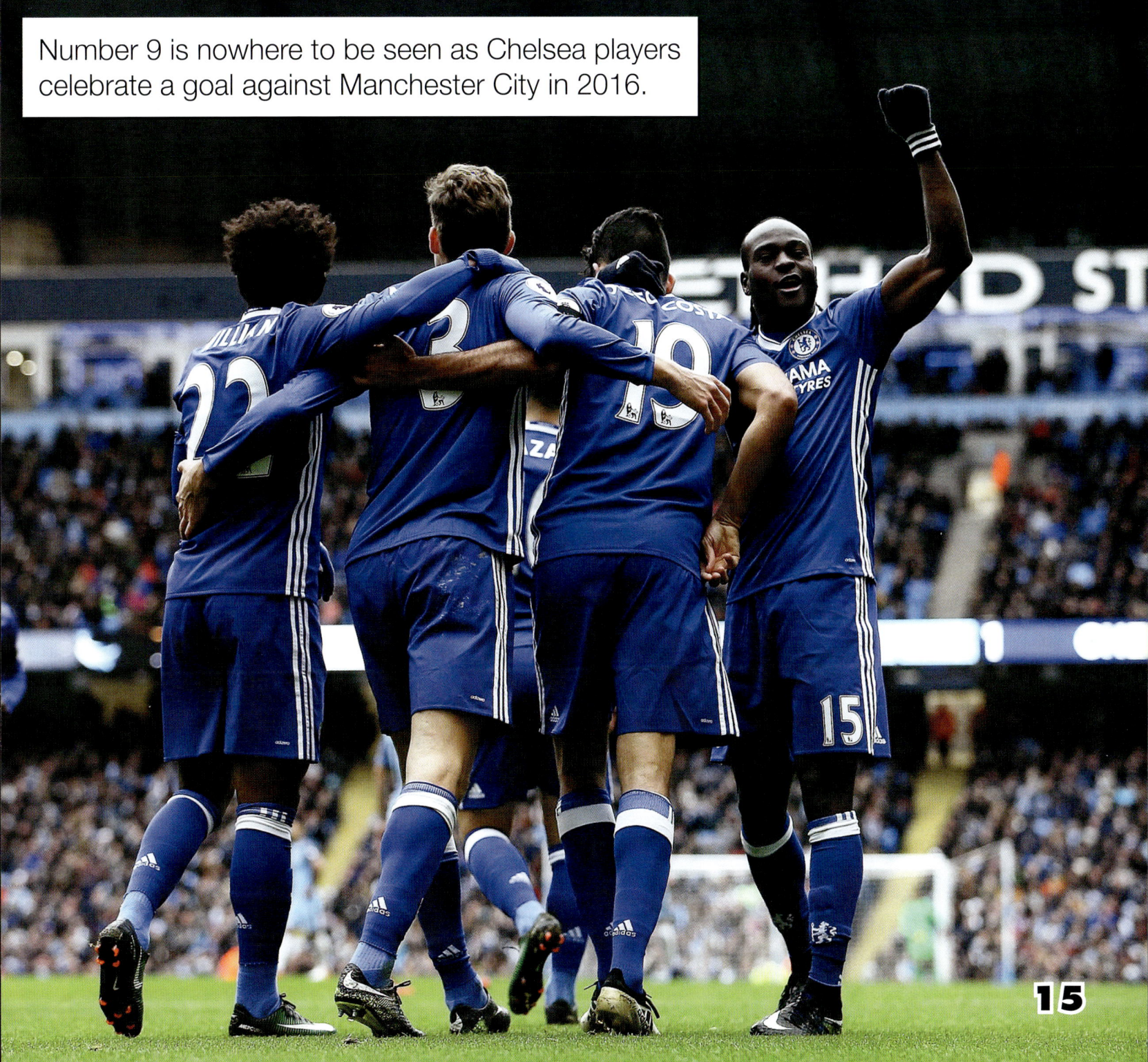
Number 9 is nowhere to be seen as Chelsea players celebrate a goal against Manchester City in 2016.

On the Map

Chelsea brings together players from all over the world. These are some of the best:

1. **Charlie Cooke** • St. Monans, Scotland
2. **Eden Hazard** • La Louviere, Belgium
3. **Petr Cech** • Pilsen, Czech Republic
4. **Fernando Torres** • Fuenlabrada, Spain
5. **Gianfranco Zola** • Oliena, Italy
6. **Marcel Desailly** • Accra, Ghana
7. **Jimmy Floyd Hasselbaink** Paramarimbo, Suriname
8. **Willian (*Willian Borges da Silva*)** • Ribeirao Pires, Brazil

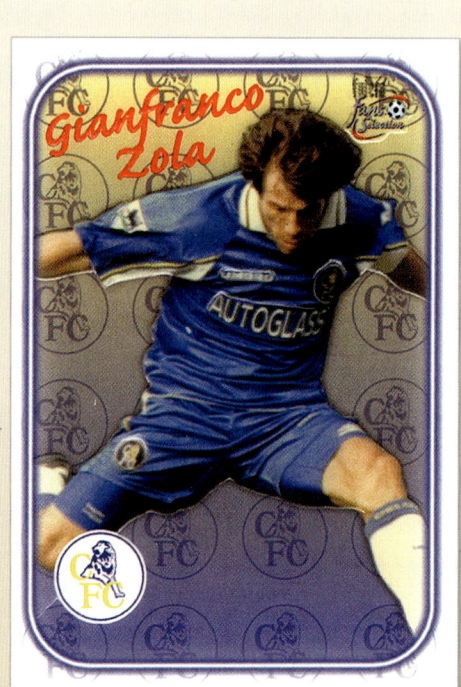

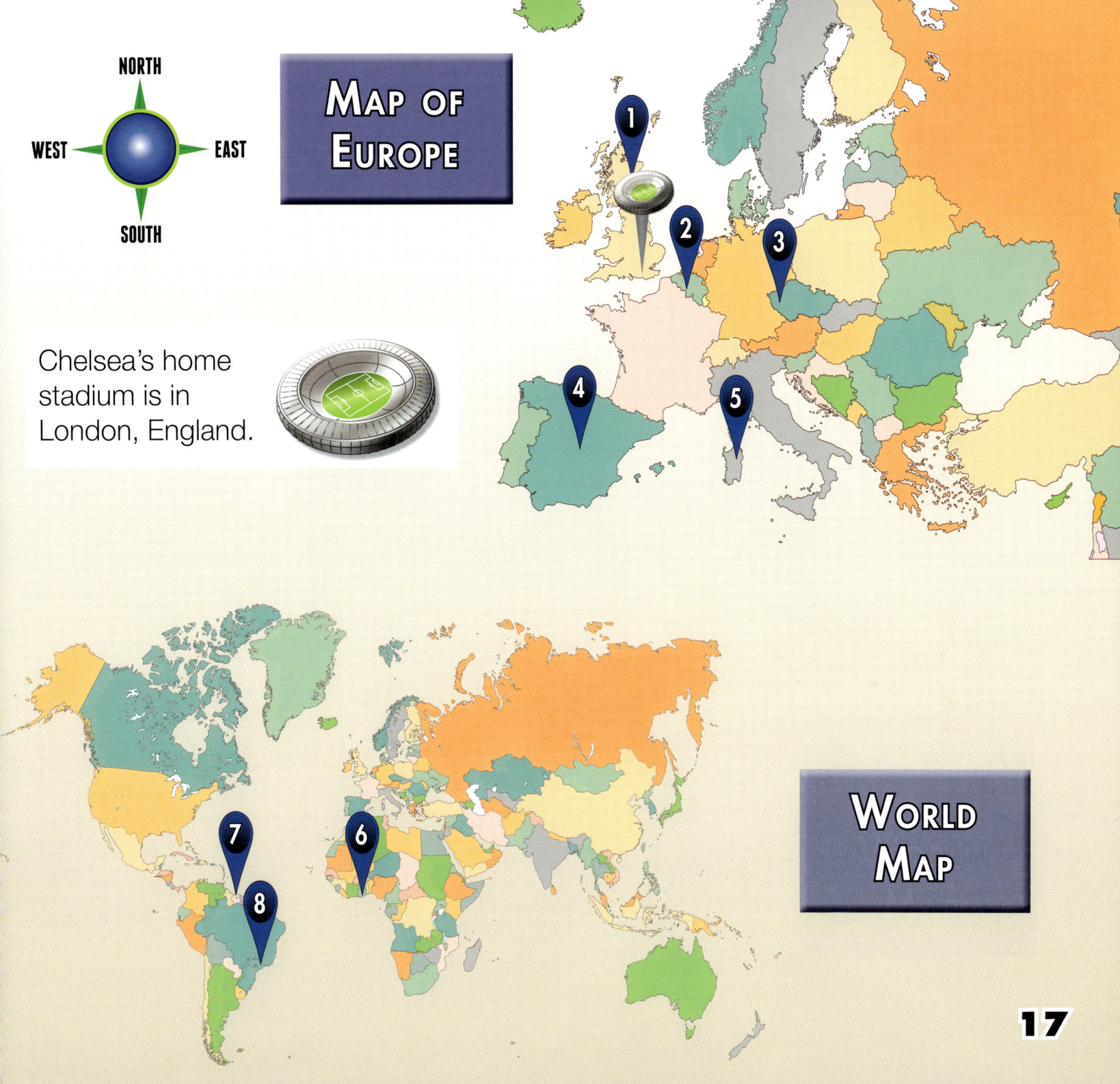

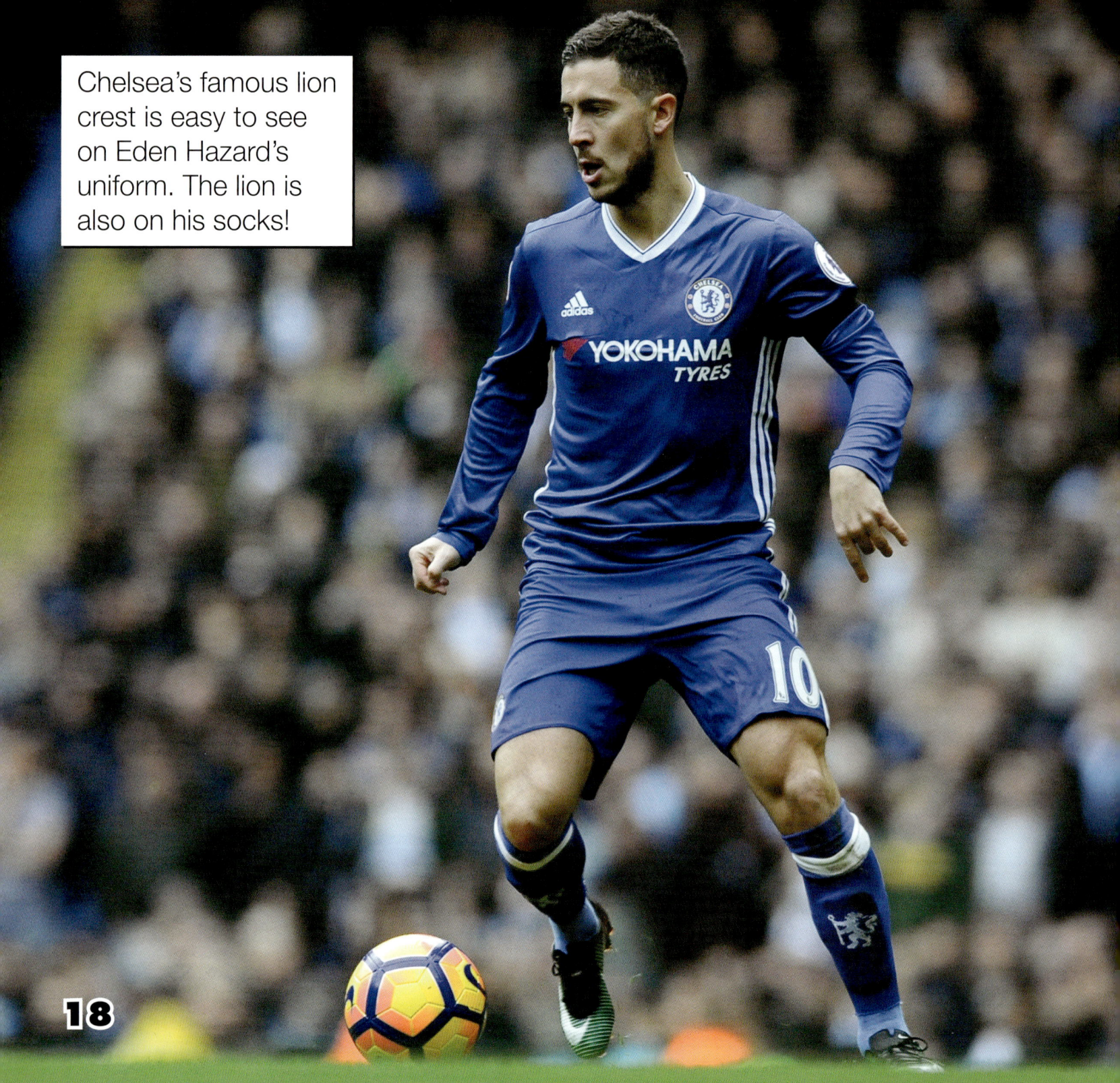

Chelsea's famous lion crest is easy to see on Eden Hazard's uniform. The lion is also on his socks!

Kit and Crest

Chelsea players have worn blue shirts on their home field since the club's first season. They have worn blue shorts for more than 50 years. Chelsea's away kit is all yellow, or white with blue trim. The team's crest shows a lion holding a staff.

We Won!

Chelsea has had many exciting seasons. None was more thrilling than 2009–10. The Blues set a league record with 103 goals in 38 matches. They needed every one, because they finished in first place by one point on the last day of the season. Chelsea went on to win the **FA Cup**. The Blues beat Portsmouth 1–0. Petr Cech was the hero. He made an amazing save of a penalty shot.

A proud Petr Cech poses with the FA Cup trophy after Chelsea's victory in 2010.

For the Record

Chelsea has won more than a dozen major championships!

Football League/Premier League

1954–55
2004–05
2005–06
2009–10
2014–15

Cup Winners' Cup

1970–71
1997-98

UEFA Super Cup

1998

FA Cup

1969–70
1996–97
1999–00
2006–07
2008–09
2009–10
2011–12

Champions League

2011–12

Europa League

2012–13

These stars won major awards while playing for Chelsea:

2000–01   Jimmy Floyd Hasselbaink • Golden Boot

2006–07   Didier Drogba • Golden Boot

2008–09   **Nicolas Anelka** • Golden Boot

2009–10   Didier Drogba • Golden Boot

2003–04   Frank Lampard • Football Association Player of the Year

2004–05   Frank Lampard • Premier League Player of the Season

2004–05   Frank Lampard • Football Association Player of the Year

2009–10   Ashley Cole • Football Association Player of the Year

2014–15   Eden Hazard • Premier League Player of the Season

23

Soccer Words

FA Cup
The championship of English soccer. FA stands for Football Association.

Premier League
England's top soccer league.

Tackler
A player who stops an opponent by stealing the ball or kicking it away.

Index

Anelka, Nicolas	23, **23**
Cech, Petr	16, 20, **21**
Cole, Ashley	23
Cooke, Charlie	11, **11**, 16
Desailly, Marcel	16
Drogba, Didier	6, **7**, 11, **11**, 23
Greaves, Jimmy	6, 10, **10**
Hasselbaink, Jimmy Floyd	16, 23
Hazard, Eden	16, **18**, 23
Lampard, Frank	6, **6**, 23
Osgood, Peter	9, 11, **11**
Schurrle, Andre	**13**
Sillett, Peter	10, **10**
Terry, John	**4**
Torres, Fernando	16
Willian	16
Zola, Gianfranco	16, **16**

Photos are on **BOLD** numbered pages.

About the Author

Mark Stewart has been writing about world soccer since the 1990s, including *Soccer: A History of the World's Most Popular Game.* In 2005, he co-authored Major League Soccer's 10-year anniversary book.

About Chelsea F.C.

Learn more at these websites:
www.chelseafc.com
www.fifa.com
www.teamspiritextras.com